MOONDANCE

FRANK ASCH

SCHOLASTIC INC.

New York Toronto London Auckland Sydney

ISBN 0-590-45488-9

Copyright © 1993 by Frank Asch.
All rights reserved. Published by Scholastic Inc.
BLUE RIBBON is a registered trademark of
Scholastic Inc.

12 11 10 9 8 7 6 5 4 3 2 1   4 5 6 7 8 9/9

Printed in the U.S.A.   23

The illustrations in this book were painted
with vinyl acrylic copolymer animation paint
on bristol board.

To Devin

One night Bear and Little Bird were sitting
outside, looking at the moon.

"You know what I wish?" said Bear. "I wish
I could dance with the moon."

"Maybe she'd like to dance with you, too?"
chirped Little Bird.

"Silly Bird," chuckled Bear. "The moon is so
   special. She wouldn't want to dance with me!"
Just then a cloud drifted in front of the moon.
"What about the clouds?" asked Little Bird.
"Would they dance with you?"
"Mmmmmm . . . maybe," said Bear.
"Why don't you ask them?"
   suggested Little Bird.

"Okay," said Bear and he called to the clouds,
"Clouds, would you come down and dance with me?"
   But the clouds stayed up in the sky.
"You see," said Bear. "Even the clouds won't come
   down to dance with me!"

Bear and Little Bird watched the sky until bedtime.

Then they said good night and went to sleep.

In the morning Bear looked out his window and
saw fog. He had never seen fog before.
"Oh, my!" he cried. "The clouds came down to
dance with me!"
Bear was so excited! He ran outside
and began to dance with the clouds.

He danced and he danced and he danced.

As the day grew warmer, the fog began to lift.

When the fog was all gone, Bear felt sad.
"Do you think I could have stepped on their toes
or something?" he asked Little Bird.
"Silly Bear," replied Little Bird. "The clouds probably
had some work to do up high in the sky, that's all."

"What kind of work does a cloud do?" asked Bear.

"Clouds make rain," answered Little Bird.

Suddenly Bear had an idea.

"Clouds," he called to the sky, "could you make some rain for me to dance with?"

Bear heard no answer, not even a rumble of thunder.

"Oh, well," he sighed. "I have my own work to do."
Bear forgot about the clouds.
He went inside and picked up his toys.
He washed the dishes and polished
all the silverware.

When Bear was finished he looked out his window
and saw raindrops falling from the sky.
"Oh, goodie!" cried Bear and he ran outside
and began to dance with the rain!

He danced and he danced and he danced.

After a while the rain stopped.

This time Bear was not sad.
"The rain got hungry and went home
to eat supper, that's all," he said.
Bear was hungry, too.
After eating *his* supper Bear went outside
and waited for the moon to rise.

For a long time Bear gazed at the moon.
"She's so special and I'm just an ordinary bear,"
 he thought. Then Bear remembered how special
 it made him feel to dance with the clouds and the rain.
"Oh, Moon," he called to the sky,
"will you please come down and dance with me?"

The moon made no reply, but when Bear looked down he saw the moon's reflection in a puddle. "Look, Little Bird!" he cried. "The moon came down to dance with me!"

Bear was so happy! He jumped into the puddle and began to dance with the moon.

He danced and he danced and he danced.

Garfield
GETS IN A PICKLE

BY JIM DAVIS

Ballantine Books • New York

Published in the United States by Ballantine Books, an imprint of Random House, a division of
Penguin Random House LLC, New York.

BALLANTINE and the HOUSE colophon are registered trademarks of Penguin Random House LLC.

NICKELODEON is a Trademark of Viacom International, Inc.

ISBN 978-0-345-52590-1
eBook ISBN 978-0-345-53754-6

Printed in China

randomhousebooks.com

10 9 8

The Geek Shall Inherit the Earth

My Laughable Life with Garfield

The Jon Arbuckle Chronicles

BY JIM DAVIS

Now Available

Accordions rule, and so — finally — does Jon Arbuckle!

It's revenge of the nerds when Jon grabs Garfield's traditional lead role and takes center stage with a delightfully dorky new book of his own.

Through classic comics, blog entries, and a wealth of other wacky new material, experience Jon's dating disasters, phone call faux pas, wardrobe malfunctions, and mirthful mishaps — and cheer the geek with a heart of gold as he finally finds true love with Liz, the veterinarian (who would've thunk it?).

So, rejoice, Jon fans, and enjoy the fun . . . the moment of *goof* has arrived!

29

GARFIELD®

www.garfield.com

JIM DAVIS 9-20

SPLOT

MY BAD

www.garfield.com

Distributed by Universal Press Syndicate

JIM DAVIS 10-25

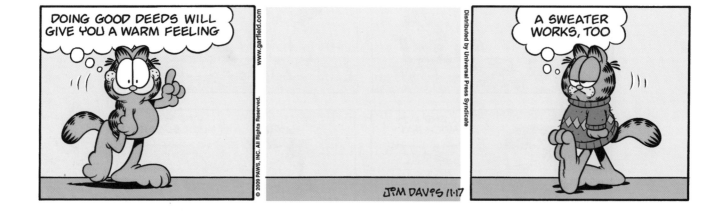

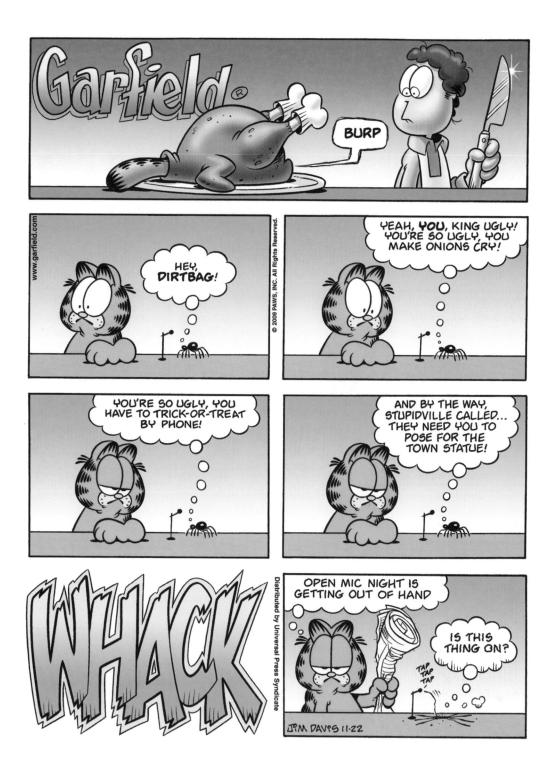

71

Panel 1: I MADE SOMETHING SPECIAL FOR US THIS YEAR...

Panel 2: SOMETHING WITH **NO** BONES...

Panel 3: TURKEY PIZZA!

I'LL CARVE!

Panel 4: THIS IS **MY** WORLD

Panel 6: CATERING BY JON

Panel 7: KNOW WHAT WE HAVEN'T DONE LATELY?

Panel 8: SCARF DOWN PASTRIES LIKE A COUPLE OF ROOT HOGS!

Panel 9: LET'S GO DOWN TO THE DONUT SHOP AND ROCK THEIR WORLD!

I LOVE THIS DREAM

Distributed by Universal Press Syndicate

www.garfield.com

JIM DAVIS 11-29

73

YOU HAVEN'T BEEN VERY GOOD THIS YEAR, YOU KNOW

WHAT ARE YOU ASKING SANTA FOR?

LENIENCY

JIM DAVIS 12-3

JON'S RIGHT. I HAVEN'T BEEN VERY GOOD THIS YEAR. MAYBE I'D BETTER START

OW

JIM DAVIS 12-4

I REMEMBER CHRISTMASES BACK ON THE FARM...

UH-OH

THE FAMILY ALL MAKING CORN COB ORNAMENTS TOGETHER...

HERE WE COME

DOC BOY HOT GLUING SEQUINS TO MY FOREHEAD...

AND THERE WE GO

JIM DAVIS 12-5

I WENT TO A GIRLY BOUTIQUE TODAY TO FIND LIZ'S GIFT

THEY HAD FANCY SOAPS, SKIN CREAMS, AND PERFUMES

THEN THIS BATTY OLD WOMAN WEARING TEN POUNDS OF MAKEUP RUNS AT ME WITH AN ATOMIZER!

I TRIED TO RUN, BUT I TRIPPED OVER A BASKET OF LUFFAS, CRASHED THROUGH A MOISTURIZER DISPLAY, AND FELL INTO A PILE OF POTPOURRI SACHETS

THEN SHE PUTS ME IN A HALF NELSON, HOSES ME DOWN WITH BODY WASH, AND FORCE-FEEDS ME BATH OIL BEADS

NOW I SMELL LIKE A COCONUT-CUCUMBER-MELON-VANILLA-CHERRY-LEMONGRASS-MANGO BREEZE

SNIFF WITH JUST A HINT OF PLUMERIA, I BELIEVE

JIM DAVIS 12-15

84

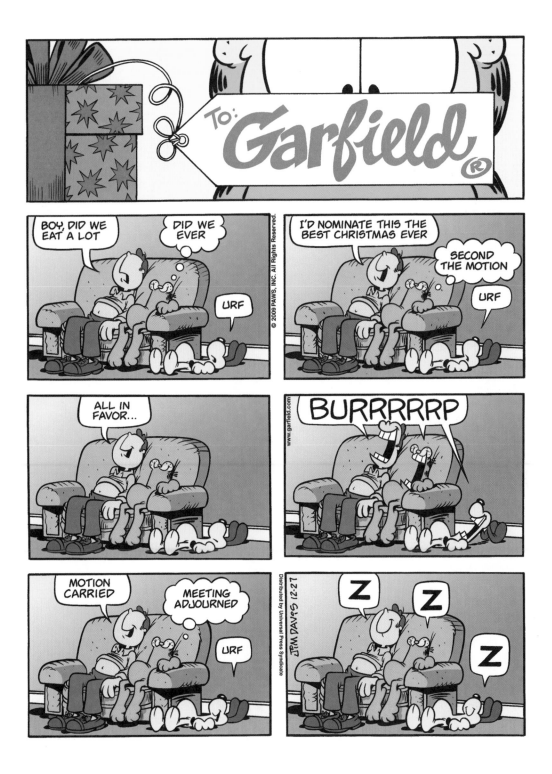